These promises are especially for

_____

With love from

_____

The Lord…is pleased with those
who do what they promise.

PROVERBS 12:22

GRANDMOTHER'S
Book of Promises

WRITTEN BY KAREN HILL   ILLUSTRATED BY DAVID CLAR

WATERBROOK
PRESS

GRANDMOTHER'S BOOK OF PROMISES
PUBLISHED BY WATERBROOK PRESS
12265 Oracle Boulevard, Suite 200
Colorado Springs, Colorado 80921

All Scripture quotations are from The International Children's Bible,
New Century Version, © 1986, 1988 by Word Publishing,
Nashville, TN 37214. Used by permission. All rights reserved.

Hardcover ISBN 978-1-57856-221-3
eBook ISBN 978-0-307-56898-4

Copyright © 2000 by Karen Hill

Illustrations © 2000 by David Austin Clar
Calligraphy by Corinne Clar

Published in the United States by WaterBrook Multnomah, an imprint of the Crown Publishing Group, a division of
Random House LLC, New York, a Penguin Random House Company.

WATERBROOK and its deer colophon are registered trademarks of Random House LLC.

Printed in the United States of America
2014
10 9 8

For Shelby
What a precious gift you are!

—K.H.

Every perfect gift is from God.

JAMES 1:17

Dedicated with love to Corinne,
who keeps her promises.

— D.C.

Come, Grandchild, come!
Please take a look—
I have something for you;
it's your own special book!
Pages of promises
straight from my heart.
We'll read them together.
Are you ready? Let's start!

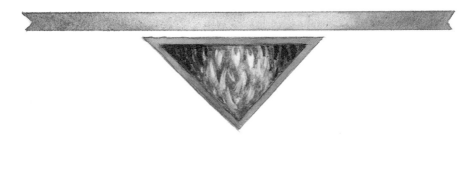

I will always love you
just the way you are.
I'll be your biggest fan;
you'll be my favorite star.
Even if your toes are chubby,
even if your clothes are funny,
I'll love you every single hour,
on rainy days or when it's sunny.

We'll plant seeds and watch them grow.
We'll feed them and weed them, and soon we'll know—
Flowers will sprout and start to bloom,
then into a vase to brighten the room.

We'll praise God together
for all that he's done.
We'll count every blessing
under the sun.
We'll thank him for family,
home, friendships, and fun.
We'll name them out loud,
every little last one.

Here's a promise for your tummy:
The food I cook will be—oh!—so yummy.
Rabbit-shaped pancakes with raisin eyes,
cookies and cocoa and maybe some fries!
All kinds of milkshakes to make our
    tongues shiver.
But I promise we'll never, ever eat liver!

I Also Promise to...

Keep track of your height on my kitchen door.
Keep your pictures on my fridge.
Always laugh at your jokes.
Help you clean up your messes.
Brush your hair and pour bubbles into your bath.

Hold these promises deep in your heart,
and remember my love for you right from the start!

When we have a crazy-dazy day,
upside down is the way to play.
I'll call you "Granny" and you'll call me you,
I'll wear my shirt backward for fun—you will too!

We'll take imaginary trips
in a cloth house made of quilts.
First it's a plane! Then it's a boat!
We'll buzz the clouds,
    and on the sea we'll float.

I'll never say, "Hurry up! Move along!"
I'll slow down with you and take routes that are long.
We won't ever rush. We'll take our sweet time,
exploring together the wonders we'll find.

We'll chase lightning bugs together
in the toasty summer weather.
We'll catch them in our hands
and feel their wings like little fans.
We'll put our fireflies in a jar
and watch their light from near and far.
After a while we'll let them go
and cheer them on as they glow, glow, glow.

I Also Promise to...

Teach you how to whistle.

Show you how to skip stones on water.

Teach you to fly a kite.

Share with you the fun of dunking cookies in milk.

Teach you all the silly songs I know!

Hold these promises deep in your heart,
and remember my love for you right from the start!

On cool, clear nights we'll count the stars
and planet hop from here to Mars.
On a make-believe cloud through the sky
   we'll zoom
and stop for a chat with the man in the moon.
We'll eat comet ice cream before we land
and dance to the tunes of the Galaxy Band.

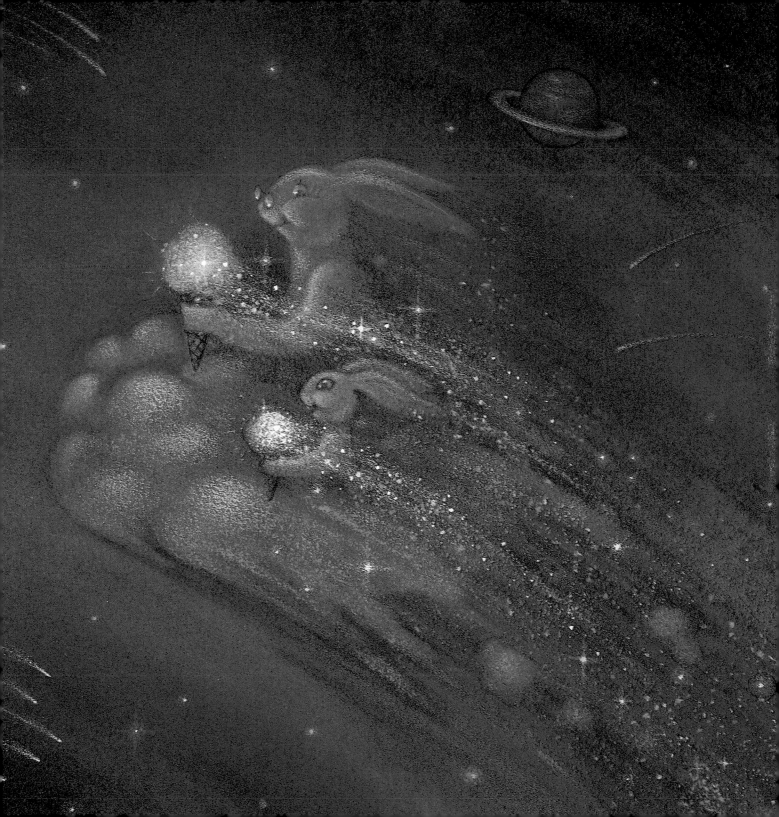

We'll have a sleepover, just you and me.
We'll sing silly songs, watch a little TV.
We'll snack on goodies, and before we're done,
we'll read stacks of books and have loads of fun.

If bedtime makes you cry,
I'll sit by your bed till your tears are dry.
I promise—if you're scared at night,
I'll sing you songs and leave on the light.

I Also Promise to...

Squirt you with the hose on hot summer days.
  (You can squirt me too!)
Make paper snowflakes with you and pretend
  we're shivering.
Take flashlight walks together before bedtime.
Draw pictures together in the sand.
Save bread crusts so we can feed the birds.

Hold these promises deep in your heart,
and remember my love for you right from the start!

On a starry night long ago,
Jesus was born (I'm sure you know).
So let's have a party to celebrate,
with a Christmas tree and a birthday cake!
We'll sip cocoa and trim the tree
as we sing about the first Christmas Eve.

For quiet time we'll snuggle together
in a big old chair, whatever the weather.
We'll read awhile, and when we're done,
I'll tell you stories of when I was young.

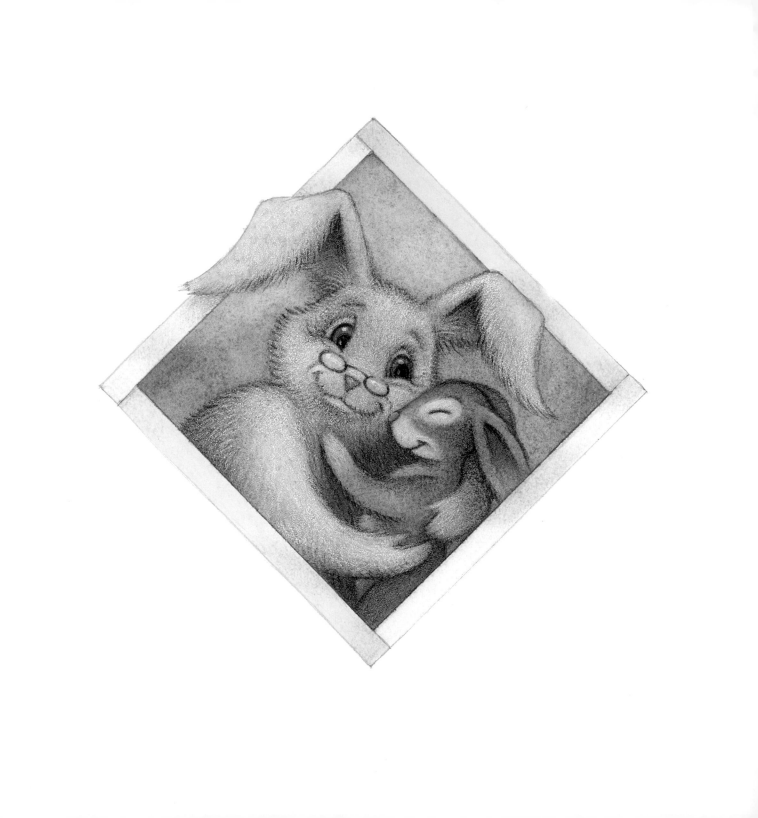

I promise to pray for you each single day.
I'll help you and love you in every way.
I'll care for you always, with all of my heart,
forever and ever, right from the start.
You're special,
   you're AWESOME,
      you're one of a kind!
Best of all, dear Grandchild, you are mine
   for all time!

Here are my own special promises for you…

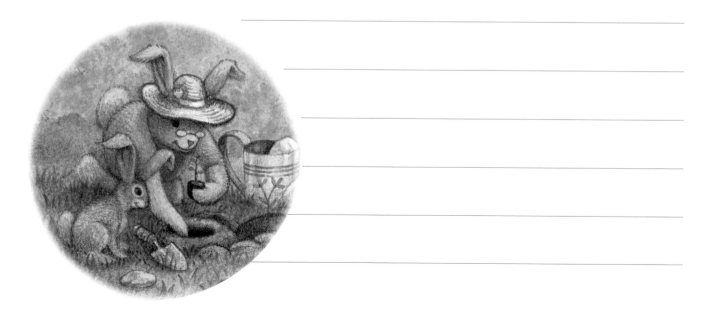

...and extra blessings to go with you into life.

Hold these promises deep in your heart,
and remember my love for you right from the start!